Jacob's Little Giant

Barbara Smucker

VIKING
KESTREL

VIKING KESTREL

Penguin Books Canada Ltd., 2801 John Street,
Markham, Ontario, Canada L3R 1B4

Penguin Books, Harmondsworth, Middlesex, England

Viking Penguin Inc., 40 West 23rd Street,
New York, New York 10010 U.S.A.

Penguin Books Australia Ltd., Ringwood, Victoria,
Australia

Penguin Books (N.Z.) Ltd., 182-190 Wairau Road,
Auckland 10, New Zealand

First published by Penguin Books Canada Ltd., 1987
Reprinted 1987
Copyright © Barbara Smucker, 1987

Printed in Canada

Canadian Cataloguing in Publication Data

Smucker, Barbara, 1915–
Jacob's little giant

ISBN 0-670-81651-5

I. Title.

PS8537.M82J32 1987   jC813'.54   C87-093520-8
PZ7.S66Ja 1987

For our youngest grandchildren,
Amy, Sarah and Aaron

Jacob's Little Giant

1

Drifting clouds hung over the farm on Beaverdale Road. Beneath them, the blanket of night folded quietly away. Softly, the gold light of sunrise crept up the sky and without a sound woke the green barns, the red brick farm house, the red tractor, the sharp-needled spruce and the ploughed fields.

The blue pond where the ice was beginning to melt still slept in the dip of earth between the fields. Its breath of mist rose and fell without a murmur.

Then from high in the sky, came a faint, wild cry. A weaving, black, V-shaped line dipped and dived toward the silent farm. The noise grew louder. The line fell through the clouds and became a hundred wild Canada geese with black necks and white cheeks glistening in the sunrise.

Jacob Snyder heard them first from the warmth of his feather-ticked bed. He kicked back his covers, jumped to the floor and pushed up his half-open window. His stiff, brown hair stuck up straight in the frosty air. Gusts of late spring snow flew onto his rumpled pyjamas.

"The Canada geese are coming from the south!" he shouted. "Hear them honking! Spring is here!"

Jacob's shouting and the honking of the wild geese shook the house. The noise woke Father and Mother. It rattled the bedroom where Jacob's older sisters, Lydia and Suzanna, slept. It pounded in the ears of his big brothers, Orie and John, in their sturdy beds in the room next to Jacob's.

Father, barefoot and in his long flannel night shirt, came running to Jacob at the open window. He closed it tight and brushed the sifting snow from Jacob's face. His own thick, grey, wavy hair was a mess of tangles and his eyes were still half-closed with sleep. He peered at the bed-room clock.

"Not so loud, little Jakie," he groaned. "It's still early. Everyone else is asleep."

"Little Jakie" — Jacob hated the name. He was only seven; everyone else in the family was bigger and older, and he wished with all his heart that he would grow.

But in spite of the name, Father and Jacob stood close together, watching the wild, beautiful creatures and their "honk, honk, honking," which was coming nearer and nearer. Their great wings beat the air and then stretched into a downward glide.

The goose that led at the tip of the V was aiming for the Snyder pond.

"He's diving for my window!" Jacob shouted again, forgetting Father's order.

"No..." He held his breath. "They're going to land on our pond!"

Father was excited, too.

Never before had the wild geese rested and fed on the Snyder farm. They had always passed over it on their hurried flight to the north and their nesting grounds on the barren shores of Baffin Island.

"Please land on our pond!" Jacob squeezed his eyes shut and hoped. The honking grew louder. The geese were coming closer. Jacob imagined himself running to the pond, putting his arms around the flagpole neck of the lead goose and flying with him over the farm house...the green barn...the potato fields...the nearby motorcycle shop...the church ...and the golf course at the end of the road. They would fly away from Beaverdale Road and Ontario and he would not come home again until he was older and bigger than all of his grown-up family. No one would ever call him "little Jakie" again.

Father squeezed his shoulder. Jacob opened his eyes, and there he was, shivering and barefoot, at his bedroom window. The geese were not landing on the pond. They were climbing higher and higher into the sky until they were only a pencil-thin V-shaped line once more.

"Why didn't they land?" Jacob shouted once more.

"Keep your voice down, Jakie," Father said impatiently. "If you can't sleep anymore, get dressed. We'll do our chores before the others wake up."

Now there were clumping noises coming from Orie and John's room. Orie, who was eighteen and as tall and strong as Father, came bounding into Jacob's room. He threw a fat pillow at Jacob's head.

Jacob ducked, and the pillow crashed into the window.

"The next time you wake me up an hour ahead of time, little Jakie," Orie's voice slurred with sleepiness, "it'll be a bucket of water on your head instead of a pillow."

Jacob knew he meant it. Orie liked order. He liked to do everything in the right way at the right time.

Mother, who managed to find some good in all her children no matter what they did, said of Orie, "He is a practical boy and a hard worker."

"Orie'd better find a wife just like him," his sister Lydia had laughed. She was twenty-one and getting ready to marry Amsey, who was also a farmer but not so practical.

Shaking his head at his sons, Father picked up the pillow and looked grim. By this time there were noises from John. They sounded like the pounding of his shoes on the floor. He was getting dressed.

Noises also came from Mother and the girls. They were clattering down the stairs and heading for the kitchen to get breakfast. Dishes began to rattle and pans began to bang.

"No more monkey-business," Father ordered, handing the pillow back to Orie. "We'll talk about all of this after chores."

Father and Orie left the room and Jacob pulled on his clothes and his heavy work shoes. He looked at his comb and then smoothed his hair down with his hands and marched down the stairs.

He wanted to ask his mother and Suzanna and

Lydia if they had heard the flying geese, but the cloud of steam from the boiling kettle hid them, and he saw Father motioning for him to hurry.

Even though the Snyder farm was used mainly for growing potatoes, there were cows and pigs and chickens in the old barn. Great-grandfather Snyder had built it over a hundred years ago when he'd moved to Ontario from Pennsylvania. It rose on a hill behind the big new potato barn, and it was one of Jacob's favourite places on the farm.

He had hiding places on the second floor where he dug tunnels in the straw. When his friend Amos came to play with him on Sunday afternoons, Father tied ropes to the barn rafters for them. They swung back and forth like squirrels leaping across swaying tree branches, then landed with a bounce in the springing straw.

Jacob's early morning job was to gather eggs in the hen house, which was in a special place on the second floor of the old barn. He tried to place each egg gently in a basket. If he broke one Mother would scold and call him a "dreamer." Father would shake his head and call him a "shussle," a Pennsylvania Dutch word that his family had used for generations.

They had brought this language with them long ago from Germany to Pennsylvania and then to

Ontario. But, even though all the older people in his family spoke the language, Jacob and his brothers and sisters didn't speak it anymore. Jacob noticed though, that whenever his parents didn't agree with each other they spoke in "Dutch." They told secrets that way, too.

Sometimes, when Jacob was gathering eggs in the morning, one or two would break. Then Orie and John would lift him in the air and throw him back and forth between them and sing, "Little Jakie better be more careful or he'll never make a farmer." Then his big sisters, Lydia and Suzanna, would come to his rescue and hold him tight and brush his stiff hair and treat him like a baby. He hated being little and always being the youngest.

But there were no broken eggs when Jacob handed the basket to Mother this morning. No one in the family liked getting up one hour early, and it was Jacob's fault. He didn't want to cause any more trouble.

2

Jacob bowed his head for Father's prayer. Father was a farmer, but he was also a deacon in the church on Beaverdale Road. Each morning he read from the big black Bible and prayed for everyone around the table.

Jacob listened, but he mainly thought about the wild geese churning their way through the sky to the faraway north. He could also smell the sputtering bacon and he could hardly wait to eat it.

Jacob liked this time in the morning with his family. It was as if they were all putting their hands together around a big, warm cup of cocoa and drinking it together, or snatching a full deep breath together before everyone jumped up to go to their jobs: Suzanna to her nursing at the hospital; Lydia to get ready to marry Amsey and move away from home; Mother to the kitchen or to her vegetable garden; Orie to all the machines in the barn, where he oiled and polished and kept them in repair; John to his agriculture classes at the university not too far away; Father to his office at the front of the house; and Jacob to school. But this week was spring break, and so Jacob never knew what he was going to do with his day. He just seemed to get in everybody's way. Still, at this time in the early morning, Jacob felt as if he were part of the family, as if he weren't so young and so little.

There was silence after breakfast, for this was when Father made announcements for the day. His blue eyes crinkled in the corners, which was a good sign. It meant that he was pleased and content. He spread his large, thick hands on the table.

"It's good we had breakfast early," he said, smiling at Jacob. He seemed to have forgotten about Orie and the pillow. "Today we plant the first seed potatoes. It's a little risky, but most of the snow is melted and the soil is warm enough. There will be plenty of time in May to plant more."

"The potatoes are cut and ready to plant." Orie scooted his chair away from the table. He

was eager to get started. "Early potatoes get premium prices, so it's worth the risk."

Jacob wasn't in a hurry. There were never any jobs for him on the big planting machine. He was too little. But he always watched. He knew that every cut piece of seed potato had to have an "eye" and that when it was covered under the ground a bud would grow from the eye. Then the bud would grow into a stem. It would spread through the earth like an underground train track. Little knobs would appear on each stem and they would become potatoes.

When Father described this process to anyone, he always said, "God moves in a mysterious way His wonders to perform." This was his favourite quotation. It came from an old poem Jacob could never remember the name of.

Father wasn't finished talking. He pushed back the grey locks of hair from his eyes and looked around the table.

"We have a little problem this morning." He cleared his throat. "We're short of help. I'll drive the tractor and Orie will keep an eye on all the machinery, as usual. But John can't help. He has an exam at the university today."

Father glanced at the girls.

"I could do it, Father," Suzanna answered in her quick, brisk way, "but I'm on duty all day at the hospital." She wore her dark hair short and clipped closely to her head. It seemed to go with her clean, white uniform, which never had a wrinkle in it. Suzanna's favourite motto was "Cleanliness is next to godliness," and Jacob didn't like it. His boots were always muddy. His fingernails were never clean enough for Suzy. He spilled food at the table when he ate. Suzanna scolded him and then in the same breath kissed him on the forehead.

Mother, who was calmer and more like Lydia, defended Jacob. "Remember, Suzy," she would say, "a home is not a hospital. Jacob is still very young."

And then Lydia, who laughed a lot and whose brown curls bounced when she shook her head, would grab Jacob and squeeze him and say, "Sweet, sweet Jakie, my favourite little brother."

Jacob liked the attention, but it also embarrassed him.

This morning Lydia laid her hand on Father's and said, "I could help too, Father, but today Mum and I are sewing on the wedding dress at Grandma's house."

Father rubbed his rough, unshaved chin and stared at Jacob.

"It is the spring break, and Jacob has no school. Maybe he could help."

"Oh, Henry..." Worry wrinkles creased Mother's wide, smooth forehead. "Jacob is still so young and the big machinery can be very dangerous."

"Well," Orie heaved a sigh. "He can't take John's place. I'll keep an eagle eye on him and he'd better keep that imagination of his under his hat."

John smiled warmly at Jacob. "I wasn't much older when I first helped with planting. I think Jacob can do it."

Jacob liked John. He was quiet and kind and helped him with his homework. He even said once that a good imagination was a special blessing, and he thought Jacob had one.

Jacob gripped the sides of the high stool on which he sat. He didn't use a chair at the dinner table because he was down so low he had trouble reaching his fork and spoon. He refused to sit on a baby pillow to make him higher.

He never dreamed that Father would let him help on the potato planter. But he knew he could do it. He knew he was big enough. He was already thinking in his mind how he would say to his best friend, Amos, who rode with him everyday on the schoolbus. "Over the holidays I rode on the planter and I poked the potatoes into the ground with a hockey stick whenever the machine missed."

Jacob knew that Amos, who was in grade two with Jacob but at least two inches taller, would be impressed.

The Snyder family scattered after breakfast like bees from a fenced-in hive. Mother knelt down beside Jacob as she tied a dark shawl over her smooth, black hair.

"Be very, very careful, Jakie. Listen to everything Orie tells you and don't let your mind wander. You are so young — so very young." She started towards the door and then turned back quickly.

"Oh, Jakie, I forgot. This afternoon Amos and his father will come for you in their car. It's Amos's birthday. They've invited your Sunday school class to their farm for a party. It's warm enough so they're going to play baseball and then eat chili. You can dress just the way you are. The planting will be finished by then." Then she was off and away with laughing Lydia and a box full of white cloth and laces. They were going to ride with Suzanna, who was sitting in her car, honking impatiently in the driveway.

Two horrible thoughts struck Jacob. What if he had had to go with the women and sit around all day while they sewed on the wedding dress?

He couldn't see why they had to spend so much time on it. Lydia was only going to wear it one day.

The other horrible thought was the coming baseball game. It was one of Jacob's favourite games. He liked to watch it. He knew all the teams and the names of all the players in the National League. But he couldn't play, no matter how hard he tried. He couldn't hit the ball. He couldn't run to the bases fast enough. He missed every catch when he was a fielder. He was never chosen to be a pitcher.

Father whistled sharply from the barn, which meant it was time to get started. Maybe the planting would take so long he would have to miss the party. But he wasn't going to think about that now. He was going to keep his mind on the planter and everything Orie said.

Jacob went into the huge, dimly lit potato barn. Last year's potatoes, sorted and washed, were bagged and piled like building blocks along the walls, waiting to be hauled in trucks to market. If it was too hot or too cold or too light in the barn, the potatoes would turn green and spongy, and nobody would eat them. None of the hamburger restaurants wanted french fries that were not crisp and crunchy.

Father was whistling far at the back of the

barn, where the machinery was kept near the roll-back door that opened into the fields. The new, red, four-row potato planter gleamed like a magic machine from outer space, Jacob thought. It had four blue cups that held the cut-up seed potatoes and the fertilizer. They could be capsules containing messages from Mars.

Orie picked Jacob up and sat him in a seat at the back of the planter. He said sternly, "See that the machine doesn't miss a planting. If it does, push a seed potato into the ground with this hockey stick. Don't wiggle in your seat and don't fall off."

The tractor was already attached to the planter. Father turned on the engine and began to drive through the open door. He waved from his high seat.

Jacob imagined that the red machine was lifting into the air, that the rays of morning sun were golden ropes tugging it upward. His eyes focused on the sky.

"Look at the ground, Jakie." Orie, who stood on a platform by the barn, glared at him.

Jacob dropped his head and stared at the ground. He must remember that this was his first grown-up job. He must put his imagination under his hat, as Orie always said. He must keep an eagle eye for any misses.

Jacob watched and watched. After what seemed like hours, he had caught only two misses. But he liked the smell of the upturned earth and the powerful pull of the tractor moving forward with Father in command. At last he was helping the family in a grown-up job.

Then he heard a honking and a squabbling above his head. He looked up. Another flock of Canada geese was heading north. They dipped down towards the pond. Jacob almost tumbled from his seat.

"Jakie!" Orie yelled. He always seemed to show up just when Jacob was doing something wrong.

The geese soared away and Jacob dropped his head. What would Orie tell Father? Would they let him help on the planter again?

At last, by the mid-afternoon the rows of early potatoes were in the ground. There would be several more plantings up to the 24th of May. Father swung the tractor towards the barn and then stopped it abruptly. He pointed towards the farm house.

"Amos and his father are waiting in their car, Jakie," he called. "You can go with them now to the birthday party."

Jacob jumped from his seat on the planter and raced towards the car. At least he wouldn't have to listen to Orie's scolding until later.

3

The birthday party was even worse than Jacob had feared. The guests were from his Sunday school class, so there were girls as well as boys. When it was time to pick captains, Amos got to be one because it was his birthday. Big, strong Millie Cressman, who always hit the ball, was the other captain.

Jacob crouched behind the other boys and girls in the open field near Amos's farm house. Jacob was the smallest one there. He was even shorter than the girls.

The captains began calling out names for their teams. Finally there were only six children left to be chosen and Jacob was one of them.

Then there were three girls and one boy who hadn't been called. Jacob was the boy. He scraped his feet over the ground and shrugged his shoulders and pretended he didn't care.

Two girls were called. Now there were only one boy and skinny little Emmie Shantz.

"Emmie Shantz," Millie shouted.

Jacob walked to the other team without even being called. He felt like crying. He felt like running home or digging a hole in the ground and crawling into it. He was sent far into the field to be an outfielder. He prayed that none of the balls would come his way. None did. When the game was over and they all went into the house, he could hardly eat the chili and the birthday cake. He didn't even want to sing "Happy Birthday" to his best friend Amos. When Mr Hoffman, Amos's father, drove him home just as it was getting dark, he didn't say a word.

"What's wrong, Jakie?" husky, red-faced Mr Hoffman asked. "Cat got your tongue?"

All Jacob could say was a small "thank-you" when the car stopped at his own house and he hopped outside.

Inside the Snyder house it was like another party. Mother, Suzanna and Lydia were setting dishes on the big, round table and cooking sausages and boiling potatoes on the stove. They "Oh'd" and "Ah'd" about the long white wedding dress that lay spread out over the chesterfield in the living room. Suzanna's friend Martha, who was Orie's girlfriend, had come for dinner.

Jacob thought Orie looked as if he had just stepped out of the bathtub and oiled his hair in the machine shop. He wore a new green suit and a shirt that buttoned so tightly around his throat that it made his face red from almost choking. He didn't even notice Jacob. He had forgotten about the morning planting.

Father was sitting under the light from the living-room lamp, with a huge pamphlet spread out over his knees. It had a sprawling picture of a red potato-harvesting machine on it. He didn't hear Jacob open the door of the room.

Jacob slid unnoticed towards John, who sat in a corner leafing through his school books.

"Hello, Jakie," he smiled. "How was the birth-day party?"

Jacob wiped his eyes and looked into John's kind gentle face. John wasn't as big or husky as Father and Orie, but he was just as strong.

"It wasn't good," Jacob mumbled. "They played baseball and I was the last one chosen."

"Oh, Jakie." John understood. He thought quietly for a long time and then said, "I'll tell you what: we'll practise ball on Sunday afternoon. I'll pitch and you hit, and we won't let anybody watch."

Jacob sighed and agreed, but he didn't think it would do much good.

The Sunday after the birthday party was a long day for Jacob. He sat in a corner during Sunday school and didn't speak to anyone. The spring snow flurries had turned into a storm and Jacob knew that he and John could never practise baseball that afternoon.

Grandfather and Grandmother Martin drove home from church with them. On Sundays Grandfather always wore his black suit and white shirt. Jacob thought to himself that he looked as stiff as a Sear's catalogue man. He didn't seem like himself until he swung off his coat and unbuttoned his shirt. After he did this, he liked to talk.

Grandfather Martin knew everything that had happened on Beaverdale Road in the last hundred years. Today he talked about the time when huge Canada geese had gathered on the Snyder pond every fall and every spring at migration times.

"They don't grow that big anymore," Grandfather sighed as he stuffed a fried chicken leg into his mouth. Jacob wondered if he would choke.

"That's what you think," Father sat up straight. There was an excited twinkle in his eyes. Everyone at the table was surprised and stopped eating.

"I was going to save this announcement until next week," Father said, "but I might as well tell you now. I've been talking to Mr McLean at the Natural Resources office up the road. They want us to raise a grown pair of giant Canada geese on our pond."

"Giant geese!" Jacob shouted, almost falling off his stool.

"Not so loud, little Jakie," Father said sternly. Jacob grimaced at "little Jakie" but swallowed his questions. In his mind, however, he began to see a goose and a gander as tall as the farm house chimney. They had feet as big as tractors, and they were padding their way up Beaverdale Road....

"He's going to bring them next Saturday morning," Father continued.

John leaned forward eagerly. He was calmer and more soft-spoken than Father or Grandfather. Everyone said he looked like Grandfather Snyder, who had died before Jacob could remember.

"When Grandfather Snyder was a young boy and lived on this farm," John said, "there were giant Canada geese nesting right on our pond."

Mother and Father, Grandmother and Grandfather Martin nodded with remembering.

"The hunters shot so many that people thought they had become extinct," John said. Extinct! Jacob thought about the dinosaurs that John had told him about. They were extinct. They didn't live anymore. Just their bones were left for people to discover under the ground.

"Well, the giant geese hadn't disappeared as all of us thought," Father's eyes crinkled merrily. "A man in Illinois found some of them in his state. He discovered that a few giant Canadas had been saved by game breeders in Michigan and North Dakota. The wildlife people of Ontario got some of them and raised more of the giants from those flocks. Now they want to settle grown pairs of giant Canadas on ponds around here, right where they once made their nests. They want us to be what they call 'co-operators' and help these pairs of giant geese to raise little giant goslings."

Little giants, Jacob thought. He couldn't speak. In his mind the giant Canadas were smashing down the potato plants and drinking all the water in the pond. Where would they swim? What would they eat?

Orie had unbuttoned the collar of his stiff

Sunday shirt, but he was still red-faced under his plastered hair. He said, "Raising geese will just add another job around here, Dad. Do we have time for them? Will it be profitable?"

"Oh, Orie," Lydia laughed. She reached across the table and ruffled Orie's neat, oily hair. "It's exciting to think that we can raise birds that were supposed to be extinct. If my Amsey and I had a pond on our new farm, we would be co-operators."

Orie whipped out his comb, straightened his hair again and gave Lydia a mean look.

"There are some things we do, Orie, without thinking about a profit," Mother said kindly. "Remember, the love of money is the root of all evil." This was Mother's favourite quotation. Jacob didn't have one yet. He thought maybe it might be, "Little drops of water, little grains of sand, make a mighty ocean and a pleasant land." It could mean that even little people were important.

Jacob remembered the time when Orie had killed a runty baby pig. Then he had said he had to do it because it wouldn't make a profit.

But Father wasn't listening. He was rubbing his chin the way he usually did when he was making a decision. He squinted across the table at Jacob.

"Jakie is still a little young to help much with the potato machines," he said.

Jacob held his breath. Was Father going to tell in front of everybody how he almost fell off his seat on the planting machine because he was looking up to watch the migrating geese?

"I think," Father went on, "Jacob can take care of the giant geese." He did not say anything about the planting.

Jacob gulped. He was pleased, but he had to admit to himself that he was scared. How could he handle giant geese? How big would they really be? Still, he wanted to try....

"I'll do it!" he blurted out. He tipped back on his stool and fell over, hitting the back of his head on the floor.

Suzanna grabbed him and felt his head. "Jakie, Jakie," she said in her crisp way. "You'll have a bump on the back of your head like a bean bag if we don't get an ice pack on it right away."

There was no way to escape from Suzanna. She made him lie on his stomach on the chester-field in the living room, with his face jammed into a pillow so he couldn't see. She put a shivery ice pack on the back of his head. Then she checked her big watch and declared that he must not move for ten full minutes. It seemed like ten full hours to Jacob.

4

The next week at school Jacob thought constantly about Saturday and the coming of the giant Canada geese. He had forgotten completely about the birthday party and the baseball game. He didn't want to talk about the geese to anyone — not even to Amos. He didn't want anyone to know that he was afraid.

When he got on the schoolbus every morning and sat next to Amos he didn't talk about his worries. Instead, he thought up riddles to ask his friend. They often did this on the way to school.

On Friday, Jacob had a good one that Lydia had told him.

"What would you grow on a farm, Amos, that was two miles long and half an inch wide?"

Jacob chuckled as he slid into the bus seat beside his friend.

"There never would be such a farm," Amos grinned with his wide mouth.

"Spaghetti!" Jacob shouted.

The bus swerved around a corner, and the boys banged together. They laughed so hard that Jacob's throat ached and the bump on the back of his head began to throb. He didn't care. It helped him to forget about the coming giants.

On Saturday the sky was flooded with sunshine. The last drifts of snow were melting along the edges in little thread-like streams.

"A good day to welcome the giant geese," Father announced after breakfast, motioning for Jacob to get up from the table and follow him.

Jacob ran to the back porch and grabbed his sheepskin jacket and cap from the hook on the wall. He pushed his heavy shoes into a pair of rubber boots that sloshed around when he walked because they were too big. The small patches of snow that were still on the ground were wet and slushy, just right for making snowballs. Jacob packed a fast one and tried to hit the barn door. It missed and landed on Father's neck.

"Jakie, this is no time for tricks." Father

brushed the snow away and peered at Jacob crossly. He took him by the hand and led him up to the old barn where the animals lived. Since it was built on a hill, they could look down Beaverdale Road from there, and watch for Mr McLean.

"He won't need his truck to haul giants," Jacob mumbled to himself and shivered. "He'll probably be riding on the back of one of them."

He stuck his hand inside Father's because it seemed safer that way. He imagined that the earth might shake under the giants' big, webbed feet.

"Here he comes, just on time," Father checked his watch. He was like Orie. He liked to have people come at the right time.

The dark green Natural Resources truck spun over the hill and down the Snyders' lane like a gliding beetle on slippery ice. Mr McLean eased the truck to a stop in front of Father and Jacob.

He seemed to be alone. Jacob looked up the road to see if the giants were coming behind him.

Mr McLean smiled calmly with his thin, fresh-air face and stuck out his long, bony hand to shake Father's large fat one. He tapped Jacob on the head.

"Hello, there, Henry," he spoke in a hearty voice to Father. "It's good to have someone like

you co-operate in this program." He stretched
his eyes over the newly ploughed black fields
and the orderly barns and the sturdy farm
house. "Good farm land is getting almost as
scarce as our giant geese. But if you keep the
geese as well as you keep your farm, they should
thrive here," he said.

For a minute Jacob forgot the giants and
thought about Mr McLean's words. Did he mean
that their farm might become extinct? He began
to imagine the golf course, the motorcycle shop,
the aluminum factory and the new houses on
Beaverdale Road all nibbling away at their rich,
fertile soil.

Father coughed and Jacob looked quickly
down the road again for the giants. Instead, he
heard a faint honking and flapping of wings at
the back of the truck. He ran behind to look.
Inside a large, wire crate were two of the largest
and most beautiful Canada geese he had ever
seen.

Their black necks rose tall and straight to the
top of the crate. Their white cheeks shone like
new snow on the spruce trees. Their soft, grey
feathers folded over their backs and their sharp,
black eyes looked straight at Jacob. They backed
away to the corner of the crate: they were wild

creatures and didn't want people too close. Could these be the giants?

Mr McLean and Father joined Jacob at the back of the truck.

"These giant Canadas are fine specimens," Mr McLean said proudly. "They're twice as big as most Canada geese. The goose weighs eighteen pounds and the gander twenty. The wing spread from tip to tip on each of them is all of six feet."

So these were the giants! Jacob's fears vanished like melting snow. He took a deep breath and filled up with warmth and pride. He was bigger than these giants and he was going to help to save them.

Jacob jumped into the front of the truck with Father and Mr McLean. They bumped over the rough road to the smooth, blue pond, where the ice had finally melted and the geese could swim.

They stopped under a tall, sweeping willow that was pale green with the promise of new leaves.

"This is the place," Father said. Mr McLean pressed down on the brakes. He nodded with approval at the willow, and the sheltering cedar and pine trees that made a wall behind it. He and Father began unloading the crate with the birds in it. They placed it gently on the ground near

the pond. Then they lifted out a large, wooden nesting box with four iron posts attached to it like the legs on a table.

Jacob watched. He stood near the geese and heard their low gabbling. They turned their heads quickly from side to side, for they were afraid of the man who had penned them into the wire crate.

Mr McLean talked with Father as they worked. Jacob listened. Mr McLean told how the geese were now three years old, how they had chosen each other as mates and would stay together as long as they lived.

The two men waded into the water in tall, rubber boots carrying the box. It had to be elevated and away from the edge of the pond, for the birds had clipped wings and couldn't fly from their land enemies.

The men pushed the iron posts into the water until they hit the pond floor. They pounded them down, deep and secure, with swinging hammers. The hammers swung higher as they nailed a ramp from the raised box into the shallow water.

Like steps on a house, Jacob thought.

The hammers didn't stop, because boards had to be nailed to two sides of the nesting box. They would be look-out platforms for the gander when he guarded his goose on her nest.

Then the men stretched a long snow fence along the shore near the nesting box. This would keep people and animals from wading into the water.

"These birds had better nest here after all this work." Mr McLean wiped perspiration from his forehead with the back of his long, bony hand. "Even with their wing feathers clipped, they might still find a way to escape. They'll hunt for another nesting place if they don't like this one. They might find another place that wouldn't be safe at all."

Jacob hadn't thought of this. Would they dig a tunnel under the snow fence and march over to the golf course? The geese were now gabbling more loudly and ruffling their wings. "Honk, Honk....HONK!" they trumpeted from their long, black necks.

Mr McLean quieted them in a soft, low voice. In the same voice he said, "Stand back now, I'm going to let them out."

Father stepped into the truck. Jacob climbed into the branches of the willow tree to watch.

Mr McLean slowly pulled up the door of the cage and let the birds out. He kept on talking to the geese as he moved the crate away from them. The giant birds ruffled their feathers in the wide, free space, then locked them back into place. They walked a few steps to the edge of the pond. There, they stretched their tall necks into the air and looked in all directions, out of wide eyes. The white patches on their cheeks glistened like marshmallows.

"We'll leave them now," Mr McLean climbed into his truck with Father. He saw that Jacob was still in the tree.

"Is the young boy all right up there?" he asked Father.

"He's fine," Father said. "He's going to take care of the geese. Some of us will be nearby if he needs help."

Mr McLean seemed surprised. "Is Jacob big enough for a job like this?"

Father said something in a low voice.

Mr McLean called softly to Jacob. "Be very quiet, young fellow. The geese get nervous if you jump around."

Jacob didn't move or speak. He didn't want Mr McLean to change his mind about leaving the giants.

"Don't get close to the geese, Jacob," he called again. "They might get mean if you bother them when they're nesting."

Jacob wanted to tell him that he knew about taking care of wild geese because John had been reading him a book about them, but he was afraid to make a sound.

Mr McLean started to get inside his truck. But then he turned and walked to the tree. He stood just beneath Jacob.

"I'll check on the pair some day soon. If they don't nest here, we'll move them to another farm."

Jacob froze with fear. More than anything else in the world he wanted the geese to stay on their pond.

At last both Father and Mr McLean climbed into the big, green truck. As the motor started Father stuck his head out the window and called.

"Come home when you hear the dinner bell ring, Jakie."

The men sounds and the truck sounds disappeared. Only the low gabbling of the geese could be heard.

Jacob was alone with the wild giant Canada geese. The potato fields and all his family seemed to disappear in the puffs of exhaust from Mr McLean's truck. Jacob began to imagine that the pond was filled with geese, that they had turned into white sailing ships with tall necks for masts, and that the wind filled their spreading wing-sails and blew them into the sky. He whistled with happiness.

The goose and the gander stared into the tree

with their bright black eyes. Jacob had frightened them with his whistling. He must remember Mr McLean's warning to be very quiet.

5

J acob whistled again, but this time as softly as a dove. The geese were alert to the smallest noise, and their black eyes stared into the tree. This pond was a strange place and they must inspect it carefully.

Jacob stopped his whistling. The geese turned their heads in all directions and began walking slowly into the water. They gave themselves a push with their huge, webbed feet and coasted around, near the edge of the pond. First their black bills skimmed off water for a drink, and then they dipped their heads into the icy pond and out again. Silver streams of water ran down their necks and over their grey-brown feathers. They paddled to the pond's edge and shook sprays of water beads into the air.

Jacob laughed from his perch in the tree. The bright eyes of the geese shot upwards. The birds stood stiff and alert.

Jacob was quiet again.

The geese began to preen and pick at their feathers. Their beaks pressed out oil from a gland near their tails and they rubbed the oil over and under each feather. Jacob knew that drops of water would glide off them now like melting snow from a raincoat. They were weatherproof. Jacob had read about this with John in the book about geese.

When the geese had finished, they glistened as though they had been polished. The gander leaned towards the goose and stroked her neck with his beak.

"He loves her," Jacob smiled. Together they walked towards the ramp of the nesting box.

Jacob hardly breathed.

The goose hopped around the box, pushing the straw that Mr McLean had piled there into the centre.

"She's going to build a nest. She likes it here. They're going to stay!" Jacob almost shouted again, but he remembered just in time to speak very softly. "They like our pond." It seemed to him that there was half a smile on the gander's smooth, black beak.

The dinner bell clanged from the house. The necks of the geese shot up like signal flags warning danger. Jacob didn't want to leave, but he had to. Mother and Father were strict about meals being eaten on time.

He slid quietly down the smooth willow trunk. He didn't want to frighten the goose and have her jump from the nesting box. Then he ran up the back road away from the pond. The gander, standing on his look-out platform, couldn't even see him there.

At the house, the big kitchen table had been stretched out longer for the noonday meal. Aunt Fanny and Uncle Ephraim had come from Pennsylvania for a visit.

They hugged Jacob. Uncle Ephraim lifted him into the air. "Jakie is a fine, strong boy even if he isn't very tall," he said.

A pain spread inside Jacob and ached against his heart. Everyone always noticed his size. He wanted to tell big Uncle Ephraim about the giant geese, but his uncle had already forgotten him. He was talking with Father about last year's bumper corn crop in Pennsylvania.

Jacob thought about snapping his uncle's suspenders to make him listen, but he knew that this would make Father cross. Aunt Fanny and Uncle Ephraim were conservative Mennonites.

The men wore suspenders on their pants and no neckties, and the women wore long, dark dresses and white prayer coverings over their hair, which they wore in buns. They believed in plain and simple living.

It's a good thing our church isn't conservative anymore, Jacob thought, noticing the slick blue jeans Suzanna was wearing and the flouncing red dress that billowed around Lydia.

Aunt Fanny, who had grown very plump, huffed and puffed as she unpacked a box of homemade jelly. Jacob spread some on Mother's newly baked bread. The jelly was bright red, with the fresh, sweet taste of cherries. Orie and John dipped some on their bread, too, and ate it as fast as they could without talking. More fields on the farm were now being ploughed for crops like barley and corn, and the older boys had to get back to work. Jacob wanted to tell Lydia and Suzanna about the giant goose walking into her nesting box, but by now everyone was in the downstairs bedroom looking at Aunt Fanny's homemade quilt. She had brought it as a wedding present for Lydia. Jacob followed them into the bedroom.

"It's a wedding ring pattern," Aunt Fanny was saying, proudly folding her hands over her large stomach. Once Jacob had seen her push a dresser drawer shut with her stomach. He was impressed.

Aunt Fanny shook the quilt out full length and spread it over the bed so everyone could see it.

Jacob leaned over to look. There were rings circling in and around all over it. They're too big for wedding rings, he thought silently. They look more like nooses for runaway steers.

While Mother and Aunt Fanny chattered, Lydia and Suzanna grabbed Jacob and brushed his hair and checked to see if his feet were wet.

"Stop treating me like a baby," Jacob muttered, but no one listened.

"I could use little Jakie in the potato barn this afternoon," said Orie, looking at Father for his consent. "He didn't do such a bad job on the planter." Jacob was amazed. Ordinarily he would have jumped up and followed him, but now he had his own important job.

"First I have to feed the geese," Jacob spoke as loudly as he could. The ears and faces of all the big people seemed high up and far away.

"Oh, yes, of course, the geese." Father seemed to find it hard to remember. "Give them cracked corn from the barn, Jakie, and then help Orie."

It sounded to Jacob as if Father were really saying, "Run along now and don't bother us."

Jacob ran. He gathered the corn from the

barn in a small pail. Then he sloshed along the muddy road in his big rubber boots far around the pond and down the back road to the willow.

He was almost afraid to look over the snow fence into the pond. What if the geese had escaped and walked away? He climbed quickly up the willow tree, holding the pail carefully so it wouldn't rattle.

He looked down and saw the geese still busy in the nesting box. The goose was turning around and around on the pile of straw, shaping a shallow bowl. Then she stood and picked down and feathers from her breast and tucked them into the bottom of the bowl where the eggs would lie.

Jacob was joyful. The giant Canada geese were nesting, and this meant they were going to stay. Jacob dipped his hand into the swinging corn bucket and let the kernels fall, plunk, onto the soggy ground below. The head of the watching gander jerked sideways. His dinner had never dropped out of a tree before. His "Honk-HONK" had a sound of surprise.

The mother goose arched her neck downward. The corn looked good to her, but she was shy and hesitant. She and the gander waited a long time before they decided to walk down the nesting ramp into the water and then swim to the edge of the pond. They had a stately walk,

Jacob thought, for their short legs were close to the centre of their bodies and they could balance themselves perfectly.

They looked at the corn, took a step forward, then lifted their heads to watch for danger. Almost faster than Jacob could see, their necks swung down and they picked up a kernel each. They pecked faster and faster until all the corn was gone.

Jacob whistled his approval. This time the giant geese hardly looked at him. They had begun to get used to his whistling.

The goose and the gander lifted their white cheeked heads as though sniffing the earth-smells of spring from the newly ploughed and planted fields. A cloud billowed into the sky and covered the sun. Snowflakes escaped from it, laughing and dancing through the air as though playing a prank with the weather. Jacob huddled against the tree trunk. The geese weren't cold. They were warm beneath their weatherproof wings.

Far up the hill, Orie waved to Jacob. He had forgotten that he was supposed to help in the potato barn. He grabbed the corn bucket and slipped down the tree. This time he ran quickly along the edge of the pond near the nesting box. The geese stiffened their necks in alarm, but they didn't hiss and they didn't flap their wings.

Just as he reached the barn he heard a car chugging towards the pond. He looked back and saw Father, Mother, Aunt Fanny and Uncle Ephraim looking out the windows and pointing at the geese. Jacob's heart pounded because he knew that his uncle had a voice like a booming drum and he hadn't heard the warning to be quiet.

But nothing happened, and they drove away. Jacob was thankful that his aunt's and uncle's visit hadn't been a long one.

In the big potato barn, a row of men and women were bent over the potato grader. A new shipment of stored potatoes had arrived. Now they were being washed and sorted by the grading machine, which had sieves for different sizes to drop through.

"You watch the moving conveyor belt for culls, Jakie," Orie directed, "and throw them in the bin."

The culls were the potatoes that were damaged, or green and scrawny and only good for pigs. It was an important job and Jacob had to keep his eyes on the moving belt every minute. He vowed to muzzle his imagination and not look up even if a whole flock of geese flew right into the barn.

6

A bright, warm sun shone over the pond the next Saturday. All the snow had melted and the rising flood waters had levelled off as though smoothed over by Mother's spatula. The pond was so calm and clear that Jacob could see schools of racing minnows near the surface. This should have made the geese happy with their new home. But when Jacob arrived with his bucket of corn, the gander was hissing and flapping his wings, and the goose was hopping nervously around her nest.

A long-eared hunting dog was bounding over the grass beside the pond, chasing a rabbit. His bark exploded in the silence, and with each bark the geese jerked their necks about, alert and fearful.

The rabbit dodged into a hole and the dog whined and circled around it. Then he stopped and turned his head towards the pond. A new scent was in the air. His sharp nose sniffed along the ground and his shaggy tail pointed straight out. He moved towards the geese like a slinking tiger.

Jacob cracked a dead limb from the willow, not caring what kind of noises he made. The dog was a hunter and was poised as if he were hunting geese.

Jacob dashed towards him, swinging the branch.

"Go home! Go home!" he shouted.

The dog stopped and pricked up his ears in surprise. No one had ever waved a branch at him before. He growled, but Jacob didn't move. He stood firmly between the dog and the geese, waving the willow branch.

The dog turned around. His ears flopped down and his tail hung between his legs. He crept away through the field.

Jacob tiptoed to the pond. The geese knew the danger was gone and they moved calmly from the nesting box. The gander peered into the tree expecting some corn.

Jacob climbed up the willow as fast as he could. He glanced down, and in the nest he saw a creamy white egg! The goose stood up, shaking her feathers. Jacob poured out all the corn from the bucket at one time and raced to the house to tell his family the good news.

Only Father and Mother were at home. They were pleased but not excited. Neither of them had time to see the egg because they had just been to the pond several days ago with Aunt Fanny and Uncle Ephraim.

"Let us know when the other eggs arrive, Jakie," Father said, patting his head as he hurried to the potato fields.

Jacob felt sad. He wanted them to share his excitement. He didn't tell anyone when four more eggs arrived in the next four days. He discovered each one after school when he ran to the nesting box after he had done his chores in the hen house. He didn't tell his family about the dog either. Mr McLean might take the geese away if he knew there was a hunting dog nearby.

Late on Friday afternoon when Jacob was sitting in the willow, Mr McLean came to check on the geese. Jacob looked fearfully over the fields, hoping the dog would not appear. Father and Mr McLean walked to the pond together. Jacob sat as quietly as he could, even though his heart was thumping wildly. Surely Mr McLean wouldn't take the geese away now. The goose sat on her nest peacefully warming her eggs.

The gander stood guard on the look-out platform.

Father was surprised. "Why didn't you tell me there were four more eggs, Jakie?"

Mr McLean was pleased. "The geese are doing just fine. They seem content and well fed. Is Jacob still watching them?"

Father laughed and pointed into the tree.

"Yes, he's watching them!"

The men walked away. Jacob felt another pain inside. They didn't seem to think his job was very important. But the geese needed him. He couldn't leave them now.

All the earth was warming now under the spring sun. Sturdy bloodroots with their white blossoms were springing from the earth. Yellow trout lilies poked up under the trees. And at the edges of Mother's garden small, red, thumb-like rhubarb shoots and tiny spears of green asparagus appeared. Stiff green reeds had begun to poke through the surface of the pond near the willow. The promise of summer blew in the sweet-smelling air. The hunting dog did not return. But Jacob did not talk with his family about the geese. They were all too busy to listen.

One day, when Father tore the month of May off the kitchen calendar, Jacob realized that the goose had been sitting on her eggs for four long weeks. Jacob was running out of patience. Even Father went to the nest to see if the goose was still there.

At last, on a warm Saturday in June, Jacob found four yellow fuzzy goslings flapping their tiny wings in the nest! He whistled with all his breath. The geese didn't fuss. They had grown used to Jacob's friendly noises.

The fifth egg was still in the nest, stirring and cracking as though it might explode. Jacob leaned far down from the tree where he had climbed onto his special branch to watch.

A tiny head pushed its way through the shell, and soon a slick, wet gosling slipped out. In minutes he dried into a soft ball of yellow fuzz. His mother looked at him and lifted her tall neck in a proud gesture.

Jacob thought the nest looked pretty messy. Then he saw the goose bend down and peck out all the sharp, cracked shells.

Jacob climbed far out on the limb to get a better look. The newest gosling was very small, and he was being trampled by his four big brothers and sisters. Could there be such a creature as a *little* giant Canada goose, Jacob wondered, and if he were so little would the Natural Resources office want to save him?

The father gander walked near his mate and peered into the nest. He seemed pleased, and he stroked the goose's long, shining neck.

"They are imprinted at birth," John had told Jacob. It meant that the goslings would become attached to whomever they saw right after they were born. That was why it was important that Jacob not get too close to the nest when the goslings were very young. It also meant that even though they were hatched in a man-made nesting box, they would know it was their home. They would come back to it after migration south and raise their own families on the Snyders' pond.

Jacob looked at the beautiful birds. He would never let them become extinct.

A shrill "peep, peep, peep" came from the nest. The smallest gosling was pushing his way to the side of the nesting box and fluffing his yellow down.

"He's as strong as his brothers and sisters," Jacob thought. "He's just little."

Suddenly the gander jumped to his look-out platform, lifted his trumpeting neck and bugled.

"Honk, honk, HONK."

A dark shadow flitted over the pond.

In the sky Jacob saw a hawk circling like a menacing spirit. Its long, curved claws hung down ready to hook into a tender new gosling.

Its sharp eyes seemed to be aimed at the littlest giant.

Jacob cried and waved a branch he broke from the tree. The goose spread her wings over the goslings and crouched low in her nest. The gander stretched his strong neck almost flat over his family, weaving it back and forth, hissing angrily with his mouth open, ready to bite.

The hawk circled more slowly. His sharp eyes saw the dangers below. He was no match for a giant goose and her gander and a small boy waving the branch of a tree. He sailed off over the tops of the tall, pointed spruce trees and disappeared.

Jacob's arms and legs shook with fright. The goslings had enemies, even on the protected pond. They needed a lot of watching, especially the littlest giant.

That evening when the Snyder family gathered around the kitchen table, Jacob told them the good news about the five yellow goslings. Everyone listened. He didn't say that one of them was very small.

Jacob even told them about the hawk. But when he told this part of the story, the hawk became almost as big as one of the airplanes he'd seen landing at the Waterloo-Wellington

Airport. He described its hooked bill as though it were as heavy as the anchor of a ship.

Mother shook her head. "You must learn to know the difference between fact and fancy, Jakie."

"Show us the exact size of the hawk." Father was cross.

Jacob measured the exact size of the hawk with both hands. John laughed. His dark hair tumbled over his head. "Jakie knows his facts," he said. "He just has a good imagination, and he was very brave to drive away the hawk."

7

A pale, timid sun shone on the farm the next morning. It gave the spruce trees a freshly painted look. It glowed on the dark red bricks of the farm house and warmed them.

Jacob was excited for two reasons. First, school was out and he had passed to the next grade with Amos. And this morning all of his family were going with him to the pond to see the goslings. But he was worried. He didn't want them to see the smallest gosling.

Hadn't Mr McLean said they were to save giant geese from extinction? The last gosling was a very little giant. He could imagine Orie wringing its neck and throwing it into the ditch because there was no profit in it.

At chore time Jacob broke two eggs when he put them into the basket. Father noticed.

"Be more careful, Jakie," he frowned. "I don't think you have your mind on gathering eggs."

Jacob didn't have his mind on the eggs at all. He was looking at Orie's fishing net with the long handle hanging on the barn wall. He had an idea and he knew he must carry it out at once.

He took the egg basket to the house and put it behind the kitchen door, being careful to cover the broken eggs. Then he ran back to the barn and walked abruptly in front of Father and pulled at his sleeve. Father was cleaning a cow stall.

"I've finished my chores, Father." Jacob was breathless. "I want to go to the pond for a minute and get everything ready for your visit." He took a deep breath.

"I want the pond to be clean and I need Orie's fishing net.... Please, Father. I'll be back in time for breakfast."

Father started to shake his head "no" but stopped in the middle. There was the beginning of a smile in one corner of his mouth.

"This time, yes," he said. "But you must hurry."

Jacob grabbed the net from the wall, filled his pockets with cracked corn and raced out the door. There was a path now from the barn to the pond and Jacob could run along it blindfolded. He was breathless when he got to the willow tree. The goose and the gander were peacefully guarding their goslings. Jacob called to them while he panted for breath.

"I've got to hide Little Giant," he said aloud. "He needs to be saved from extinction, too."

Jacob sprinkled kernels of corn on the ground. The goose and the gander jumped from the nesting box and swam towards him. Then he held the big fishing net high over the nest. He swooped it down on top of Little Giant and lifted him into the air, peeping and twisting.

Jacob ran far from the pond and the road. He didn't want the big geese to attack him. He ran to a tall patch of waving grass and gently dropped the net and the gosling in the middle of it.

"I'm sorry, little gosling," Jacob said, leaning over the frightened crumpled creature, "but I have to hide you."

Next, Jacob ran for the snow fence that lay on the ground nearby because it wasn't needed anymore for protection. He stood it up in a circle around the captured gosling. He untwisted the net and dropped the little yellow gosling in the grass. He left the net beside the young goose.

"Nothing will hurt you," Jacob whispered, "and I'll be back in a hurry."

Within minutes Jacob was in the kitchen nervously eating breakfast with his family.

"Why don't we all drive to the pond in the pick-up truck?" Orie suggested. "We can drive up the back road and not scare the geese."

Father said this was a good idea. It would save time. His Bible reading and prayer were short, and Mother decided to wash the breakfast dishes later. Jacob hoped with all his heart that they wouldn't notice the snow fence standing in a circle in the tall grass.

Orie drove with Father and Mother in the front. Suzanna, in her starched nurse's dress, Lydia, John and Jacob piled into the back. They bumped down the narrow back road near the spring-fed stream that emptied into the pond until they came to the willow tree. No one but Jacob looked in the direction of the snow fence. When they neared the pond he warned everyone not to make a sound.

The family climbed out of the truck and looked down at the nesting box, but the geese weren't in it. Four fuzzy goslings were swimming in a line around the pond. The gander proudly paddled in front of them and the goose, looking nervous and ruffled, was at the rear.

She was troubled because the little gosling has disappeared, Jacob knew.

Jacob whistled with surprise when he saw the others swimming. "How can they swim so soon?" he cried. "They haven't been hatched very long."

"It's a miracle," Mother smiled. The others agreed.

"I thought there were five goslings," Father pondered.

"Maybe the fifth one wasn't ready to swim yet," Jacob suggested weakly.

"Well, let me know when he starts, Jakie." Father scanned the pond. Jacob hoped he would forget about the missing gosling when he got back to the potato fields. Today they were digging the first potatoes that Jacob had helped plant in the early spring. The fields that had been planted later stretched to the sky with leafy green plants and hundreds of white blossoms sprinkled over them. The others weren't alarmed about the missing gosling.

"They do look big and healthy," Orie speculated. "It's good that you feed them corn every day." Jacob held his breath. What if the little gosling, who was not so healthy looking, began to honk in the nearby grass?

"They are beautiful." Lydia clasped her hands together and swayed back and forth with a dreamy look on her face. "When Amsey and I get married, Jakie, you can give us one of the goslings for a wedding present."

"But you don't have a pond," Jacob protested.

"I'll put it in a washtub," Lydia laughed, shaking her bouncing curls.

"She's just joking," John whispered, noticing Jacob's concern.

Suzanna patted Jacob's head. "The goose does a good job keeping her goslings clean," she said and then swatted a mosquito on Jacob's neck so hard that it made him jump.

Father seemed pleased with the swimming geese, even though he didn't say it. He checked his watch and decided it was time to leave. They all climbed back into the pick-up truck.

"I'll stay here," Jacob said, trying to sound a bit bored.

"It must be a little lonely for you here, Jakie." Mother looked towards the farm house, but couldn't see it because the leaves were thick on all the trees now and blocked off the view. "I'll invite Amos to come over and he can watch the geese with you."

She climbed into the truck with all the others, and they drove away.

Jacob didn't want Amos to come and see the geese. Amos wouldn't understand about being quiet and it would take the geese and the goslings weeks and weeks to accept him. Besides, Amos might tell about the runty gosling. He wasn't good at all about keeping a secret.

Jacob waited until the truck was out of sight and then dashed to the hiding place in the tall grass. He looked inside the snow fence barricade. The small gosling was asleep on top of the fishing net.

He's probably worn out trying to keep up with all his big brothers and sisters, Jacob thought. He picked the net up slowly and carried it with the gosling back to the pond. Little Giant didn't stir. Jacob placed him on the shore and then ran back to get the snow fence and put it near the pond again. He scurried to the willow and climbed onto his branch.

The splashing of wings and a chorus of honking told Jacob that the little gosling had been found. He could see him swimming directly behind his brothers and sisters. The goose, at the end of the line, seemed serene and happy.

"He can swim!" Jacob was amazed.

Mother did call Amos, and that afternoon he arrived. Jacob had to admit that he was glad to see his friend's round, jolly face. But he had

warned Mother that the geese were a secret and that Amos was not to know about them.

"We'll go fishing," Jacob announced. He pointed to two long bamboo fishing poles with lines, hooks and reels attached to them. They were propped against a tree. He showed Amos a can of fresh plump worms that he had just dug from the swampy area below Mother's garden.

"You've sure decided everything fast," his friend grinned.

The two boys picked up their poles and the bucket of worms and headed for the end of the pond that was opposite to the nest. They couldn't see the geese from there.

"Orie saw a pike up here about a mile long." Jacob stretched out both arms as far as they would go.

"Only a mile?" Amos laughed.

They found a dry place along the bank, baited their hooks with wiggling worms and threw out the lines as far as they would go.They waited and waited. Amos tried to tell a riddle, but he couldn't remember the punch line. Jacob pretended he was going to push him in the water unless he thought of it.

Suddenly Jacob's line jerked and he almost dropped it. A huge tug from his hook pulled him into the water. He wasn't strong enough to hold it.

"Help me, Amos!" he cried.

Amos dropped his own pole and both boys grabbed the one that was swaying and bending.

A long, angry fish flipped out of the water for a second. Rows of yellow spots gleamed on its slick, green skin.

"It's the pike!" Jacob screamed. "It's the mile-long pike!"

At this moment, just behind Jacob, a dog growled and barked. Jacob turned to look and saw the hunting dog. It was the one that had tried to attack his goslings weeks ago. He had to chase him away at once.

Jacob forgot Amos. He forgot his fishing pole. He forgot the pike. He grabbed a dead stick from the bank and rushed after the dog, which at first stood his ground but finally began to run towards the road.

When Jacob returned to Amos he saw that the pike had gotten away. The bamboo pole that had held it was split through the middle. Amos was stamping up and down in anger.

"Some friend you turned out to be, Jacob Snyder," Amos choked on tears that he tried to wipe away with a dirty sleeve. "You left me alone with your pole to chase some stupid dog. We could have caught the biggest fish in the history of this pond."

Amos began fastening his boots tighter and pulling his stocking cap down over his round head.

"I'm going home. I'm going to walk home. I'm not coming over here again for the rest of the summer." Amos stamped away towards the road.

What could Jacob do? How could he explain to Amos or to anyone in his family why it was more important for him to chase the dog away than to catch the "biggest fish in history"? Amos meant what he had said about not coming over again all summer. Jacob wouldn't even see him in Sunday school. There were no more Sunday school classes until September.

8

J acob missed Amos. There were no other boys his age who lived nearby and all the relatives and friends who came to visit had grown-up children.

Jacob thought of riddles he wanted to share with Amos. He wanted to try fishing with him again for the mile-long pike. It was no fun fishing alone. He might even show him the geese now that they were growing, and tell him about Little Giant. He would call Amos and ask him to come over this afternoon. He ran to the phone and dialed the Hoffmans' number.

Mr Hoffman's jolly voice answered.

"I want to talk with Amos," Jacob said in an urgent voice.

"Why, Jakie," Mr Hoffman's voice slid upwards

with surprise. "Didn't Amos tell you? He and his mother have gone to Alberta to visit. They won't be back until the beginning of school."

Jacob hung up the receiver without saying another word.

He didn't have a best friend anymore and he also had a worry that nibbled at his thoughts day after day.

Even with all the good things that were happening, like warm weather coming, and getting to go barefoot, and hitting a home run when he practised baseball with John in the evenings, the worry wouldn't go away.

The goslings were a month old now and covered with greyish, grizzled hair. Their first feathers were beginning to sprout. Four of them were already half as big as their parents, but not Little Giant. He was still much smaller. When Jacob sprinkled corn along the bank Little Giant ran to get it, but by the time he got there the corn had already been eaten by his big brothers and sisters.

Mr McLean was due for an inspection visit anytime. There was no way Jacob could catch the smallest gosling and hide him now. He didn't talk with his family about the geese anymore. He didn't want them to make another visit to the pond.

After breakfast on a bright summer morning, Jacob walked slowly along the pond, jiggling a fresh bucket of corn. As he neared the nesting box, he heard the goose and the gander gabbling and honking with low, nervous noises. He raced to the pond.

A gosling was missing! Jacob counted only three big goslings and Little Giant. He felt sick, for along the path to the upper road he saw drops of blood and a scattering of small, grey feathers. There were wet tracks in the damp mud and Jacob knew them at once as the tracks of a fox. He had seen fox tracks before near the old barn where the animals lived. If only he were bigger, he would get the hunting gun and shoot him. Jacob sat quietly in the grass rubbing his eyes to keep the tears from coming.

John found him there when he walked from the upper field where he was working. He saw the fox tracks and counted the goslings and he knew at once what had happened. He didn't seem to notice Little Giant.

"He's a sly old fox and he was hungry," John said.

"But he might eat all the geese. Then they would be extinct," Jacob said in a fearful whisper.

John was serious. "The goose and the gander have been warned now. They know how to protect their goslings. Their wings are like steel and their bills are as sharp as butcher knives."

Jacob felt a little comforted.

"And besides, Jakie, they have you to help them."

John tousled Jacob's hair.

Jacob remembered how the goose and the gander had frightened the hungry hawk and how he had chased the hunting dog away. Little creatures needed a lot of care and protection. It wasn't easy to save something from becoming extinct.

That night at dinner he told his family the sad story about the fox eating one of the goslings. He started to say that the fox was as big as the willow tree with eyes that glowed like bonfires. But he remembered just in time about the fact that foxes on their farm were no bigger than a small dog.

"I'll get that fox," Orie promised. For once Jacob was glad that Orie was his brother.

"Little Jakie is a good goose watcher," Father said.

"Don't call me 'little Jakie,'" Jacob protested loudly.

The green, growing month of July ended. The

Snyder farm exploded with work: in the potato fields and in the barn, in the apple orchard, in the vegetable garden, with the animals. Jacob's help was needed now, and he raced to the pond between chores. He missed Amos every day and he wished that he would write. But no letters came.

The three big goslings were growing as tall and beautiful as their parents. Little Giant looked like them, too, but he was still much, much smaller. He might never grow to be a real giant, Jacob decided. Mr McLean hadn't come yet for the next inspection trip. Jacob dreaded it.

One day he had a new idea. He threw only part of the corn to the big geese and waited until they had finished and paddled into the water. He whistled in a low and friendly tone to Little Giant and sat on the ground, holding out some corn in his hand.

"Little Giant," he called as softly as he could. "I don't care if you're little. You have a long neck and nice white cheeks. You're strong. Come...Eat the corn in my hand."

Little Giant cocked his head nervously from side to side. His dark, bright eyes looked straight at Jacob. His black, webbed feet stepped hesitantly forward. He waddled closer. His neck swung down. Peck! He gobbled one kernel. Then he moved away, as if he were suddenly afraid because he had been so close to a creature who wasn't wild.

Jacob's heart thumped with excitement but he didn't move.

"Come, Little Giant," he called again. "Eat some more corn."

This time the gosling came forward with a low gabbling.

"I'm not afraid," he seemed to say.

He pecked at Jacob's hand. Jacob slowly lifted his other hand and stroked the smoke-coloured feathers that were growing on Little Giant's back. The gosling looked quickly at Jacob, then turned around and splashed into the water.

Jacob felt warm and glowing like a candle flame inside a crystal glass. The wild gosling had eaten from his hand and he had touched his soft feathers. Little Giant trusted him. They were friends.

Little Giant paddled across the pond to join his family. He was almost there when he skidded to a stop in the water and swung around, looking intently up the back road. There was a faint noise of a humming motor and bumping tires.

Jacob heard it, too. He scrambled for the willow and climbed as high as he could in the branches. A strange, scratched-up car, faded blue like an old work shirt, was creeping up the back road. Jacob could just barely see its rusted licence plate. The car stopped beside the willow. Two men, whom Jacob had never seen before, slowly creaked open the car doors, leaving them both ajar. Each man carried a gun. A prickly fear ran up and down Jacob's legs and arms.

The men crept towards the willow trunk and crouched down on their knees. They lifted their guns and aimed at the giant gander. Jacob tried to shout but no sound came from his throat. He couldn't move.

But Little Giant was not quiet. He honked high and shrill. His sharp eyes focused on the willow tree. He churned up bubbles of water and paddled towards the gander, then slipped in front of him as though forming a shield.

"Don't shoot!" Jacob's voice began to work. He threw down the bucket filled with corn. It fell on the one man's head. Corn spilled over the other man's shoulders.

"BOOOMMM!" A blasting noise roared through the air. Pellets of shot sprayed over the road. Jacob had ruined their aim, but one of the geese had been hit.

"You shot my goose!" Jacob slid down the trunk without any thought of danger. "It's against the law to hunt giant Canadas."

From a nearby potato field, Orie had seen the strange car and the two men with their guns. He stopped the tractor and raced towards the pond. Near the barn, Father and John jumped into the pick-up truck and roared at top speed down the spruce lane towards the back road. Mother had called Mr McLean at the Natural Resources office when she heard the shot. He jumped into his green truck and sped towards the Snyder farm, racing the engine. Lydia ran from the garden with her apron flapping in the wind.

The gander honked and hissed, calling the goslings into the reeds. But the goose swam around her youngest gosling. Little Giant had been hit by a pellet!

The two strange men stared at Jacob in disbelief. They lowered their guns and ran for the car. They jumped inside, started the motor and sped away.

Jacob scrambled down the bank towards Little Giant. Tears ran down his cheeks. The gosling's proud neck seemed to dip about awkwardly. His honkings were filled with fear and pleading. The pellets had torn one of his new feathers, and blood ran over his smoke-coloured back. His mother guided him to the edge of the pond.

Father, Orie, Mother, John, Lydia and Mr McLean began to arrive. They stood near the willow looking down at Jacob and the geese. Jacob told them what had happened — how the smallest gosling had paddled in front of the big gander and saved his life.

Mr McLean noticed that Jacob stood very near the injured bird while he talked and that the gosling was not afraid of him. The tall Natural Resources man carried a long-handled dip net in one hand. He slowly pulled a wire crate through the grass with his other hand. He motioned for the others to stay far back from the pond.

He called to Jacob. "Talk quietly to the geese. They trust you."

"We're going to help you, Little Giant," Jacob said softly. "Mr McLean wants to save you, too."

Mr McLean's long, slim hands gently dropped the net over the injured gosling. And before the gander had time to attack, he popped the wire cage on top of Little Giant. He slipped it away from the pond's edge and carried the cage to the truck.

"Poor little fellow. He's terrified." Mr McLean peered through the wire. "But I think it's only the wing that's injured."

Then he looked closely at the gosling. "He isn't as big as the others." He seemed surprised. "This doesn't happen very often."

Jacob was terrified. After all, the man only wanted to save *big* giant Canada geese from extinction.

Mr McLean became more serious. "There's a large fine for anybody hunting giant Canada geese in Ontario," he said.

He bit his lip and squeezed his hand into a fist. "You can tell us about the car, Jacob, and how the men looked, but unless we know their licence number we'll never be able to catch them."

"Oh, I know the number. I saw it from the tree," Jacob answered simply. He carefully recited the numbers and letters.

Mr McLean stared at Jacob and wrote the licence number in a black book.

"You are a smart young boy," he said.

Then he started the motor of the truck to take the injured gosling to the Natural Resources office.

9

Two days passed and there was no word from Mr McLean. Jacob was so worried he couldn't eat much. His stomach felt sick. He went to the pond to feed the three big goslings and the goose and gander, but when he saw the empty place where Little Giant should have been, he had no heart to be near the others. He climbed high into the willow mainly to watch down Beaverdale Road for the green Natural Resources truck to come. He remembered over and over how Mr McLean had noticed that Little Giant was smaller than the others.

John played ball with Jacob almost every evening and he was getting better, but he didn't care too much. All he could think about was Little Giant.

The geese swam close together now, and hid in the reeds more often. Jacob knew that they missed Little Giant, too. It was the end of molting time for the goose and the gander. All their worn-out feathers and their clipped flying-wing feathers were falling off like dried leaves. They were growing new feathers, just like their goslings, and soon, for the first time in their lives, they would be able to fly. They would no longer be earthbound. No one would clip their wings again. They would be free to fly wherever they wanted to go. Jacob watched them preen and pick at themselves under the hot sun.

Jacob wondered if Little Giant's feathers were growing. He couldn't bear to think that he might never come back to the pond, that he might never learn to fly.

More days went by. Jacob sat at the breakfast table one morning and picked at his eggs and bacon. Mother was worried and patted his hand. Father said there were still three goslings left and that was a good number. But Jacob couldn't explain about Little Giant and how he was the only one who had eaten from his hand and let him touch his smooth, grey feathers.

After breakfast Jacob walked slowly to the pond with his rattling bucket of corn. The geese were gabbling and honking as though there was danger again. Jacob grabbed a large stick and raced though the tall grass. There was no dog barking, there was no hawk circling in the sky. Orie had trapped the fox two weeks ago. But there was a green truck parked by the willow tree.

"The Natural Resources truck!" Jacob cried. The tall figure of Mr McLean was leaning against it. There was a wire crate in the back, but it was empty. Jacob looked in the pond and saw three big goslings and Little Giant. He was paddling far behind the others, but he was swimming.

A burst of wondrous beauty filled all the summer earth for Jacob. The rows of green potato plants in the fields became a magic carpet. A bright red cardinal that streaked across the blue summer sky and landed on a swaying limb in the willow became a messenger from the moon. The bird sang a cheerful song that ended with upward notes that were carried in all directions with the wind.

Mr McLean called to Jacob from the truck.

"The gosling will be fine," he said. "One wing is slightly torn but it will heal. We banded him on his left leg. Now he has a number and date and we can trace his migration route. He isn't as big as the others — but, well, he's a brave little giant."

Jacob wanted to shout and whistle with happiness at the same time.

Mr McLean's eyes stretched over the gently rolling farmland.

"The geese like it on your pond, Jacob. I hope your father will always keep this farm. They'll survive here."

With that he climbed into his truck and drove away, leaving Jacob alone by the pond.

A loud splashing came from the water. The gander was testing his strong, new wings. He skittered in half-flights across the water, his feet making two rippling paths as they dangled beneath him. The goose spread her wings and flapped at the air as though climbing an unseen ladder. Their wings lifted them off the ground.

Little Giant didn't try. He seemed to be watching fearfully with his bright black eyes. Jacob walked quietly to the pond. He held corn in his hand for Little Giant. He was becoming a beautiful gander. His smooth, oiled feathers lay flat over his back, and the frayed edge of his injured wing could hardly be seen.

Jacob whistled a welcome. Little Giant swerved about in recognition. He swam slowly forward, but there was still fear in the twitching of his neck.

"You saved your father's life, Little Giant."

Jacob tried to soothe the fear in the wild bird's eyes. "Your wings are smaller, but your eyes are sharper than the others'. You can fly, too. Just try harder."

A whirring of wings broke the silence. The big gander sailed above them. His wide, spreading wings beat the air faster and faster and lifted him high into the air. The goose trailed behind him, honking with the joy of flying in the air after three years on the ground with clipped wings.

"They swim through the air," Jacob said aloud. He yearned to fly with them. The three big goslings were like their parents, arching and thrusting with the same perfect rhythm.

Little Giant stretched his long neck towards his family. Painfully, he spread out his injured wing. He could at least flap his wings like his brothers and sister.

Jacob watched, trembling and hopeful.

Little Giant flapped harder. His feet lifted from the surface of the water! But he only skimmed the water, then splashed back into the pond.

"You can fly, Little Giant," Jacob cried from the bank. "You can lift yourself into the air!"

The dinner bell clanged from the house. Jacob ran through the blue grass, stretching out his arms as though they were wings. He was flying towards the house, he imagined, and floating into the kitchen. He could hardly wait to eat the bean soup that Mother ladled into his bowl. He ate without stopping and drank huge gulps of milk.

"Has the gosling come back?" Father asked, his eyes crinkling into a smile.

"Oh, yes!" Jacob exclaimed with his spoon in mid-air. "And now he can fly as fast as the jumbo jet from Toronto."

"Our facts and Jacob's fancies." Mother sighed and shook her head.

"Well, not that fast," Jacob lowered his spoon into the soup again. "But he can get his feet off the ground."

10

Tiny swirls of cold air crept through the summer breeze and the sun seemed to hurry faster across the sky. Sometimes in the early morning, hoarfrost stiffened the grass until it prickled with cold against Jacob's bare feet. He decided to put on some shoes.

The geese flew higher and higher each day. Little Giant tried hard to keep up with them, even with his injured wing. Now he could climb into the air as high as the tallest branch on the willow. He couldn't fly like a jumbo jet, but he could land like one. When he saw the other geese floating downwards, then gliding through the air, he joined them. They soared down through the sky, winging low. Their webbed feet dropped like airplane wheels and they braked against the wind with their wings. They skidded along the surface of the water and then stopped. All of them lifted their long necks and looked proudly at Jacob.

Jacob felt a burst of happiness, but there was also a sadness hiding deep inside him. He loved the geese, but they were wild. They liked the food he brought them but did they truly love him? They would never play with him or talk with him or really be his friends. And when it was fall, they would fly away. He wanted a real friend again. He wanted Amos to come over so he could show him the geese and he wanted his family to come to the pond again and see how he had helped to save the giant Canadas from extinction.

But Amos wasn't at home and Jacob's family was so busy — they seemed to have forgotten about the geese and even about him. They just muttered things like, "I see the geese are flying" or "I noticed that the injured gosling managed to get into the air."

Jacob kept on practising baseball with John. He hadn't grown much taller during the summer, but he had become stronger, and sometimes he gave the ball a flying hit, even though he never struck another home run.

"Next year when Amos has his birthday party

and they play baseball, you won't be the last one chosen for the team," John promised.

Jacob wondered if Amos would even invite him to his party.

Then, one day near the end of August, a change took place on the Snyder farm. It was as though a storm had struck and halted all the everyday activities. Jacob forgot to scatter corn for his growing geese for two days in a row.

It was time for Lydia's wedding.

Relatives came from near and far. The house was cleaned from basement to attic and the yard was so neat and clipped that it didn't look real. Every weed had been plucked from the flower beds and the vegetable garden.

At breakfast, after family worship, the Snyders talked about clothes instead of farm chores. Jacob and his father rode to the nearest shopping centre and bought new suits. Mother's new electric sewing machine seemed to stitch at lightning speed as she lengthened Father's pants and shortened Jacob's.

Lydia's white dress hung in her closet with sheets around it, and Suzanna, who was going to be the maid of honour, sewed for a whole day and through the entire night and made her own dress of shimmering blue. Orie and John got new haircuts at a barber shop and Father sat

Jacob on a high stool and clipped his hair so short he didn't have to comb it. Suzanna said he looked like a skinned rabbit; Orie thought his hair was more like stubble on a harvested wheat field. But Lydia kissed the top of his head and said it was as soft "as the down of a goose." That pleased Jacob.

The wedding would be in the church late Saturday afternoon and everyone in the church was invited. Jacob was excited about the invitation. He would see all the boys and girls from his Sunday school class except Amos, who wouldn't be home in time.

The wedding day arrived. The sunlight sparkled along Beaverdale Road, and some of the leaves on the maple tree had already turned to "dripping gold," as Lydia said.

Baskets began to arrive in the church basement. They were filled with freshly baked cakes, pies, bread, pickled beets, newly picked cucumbers and tomatoes, slices of home-cured ham and a huge wheel of cheese from Uncle Menno's cheese factory. They were whisked up by the women of the church, who were preparing the wedding lunch. The basement had been transformed into a dining room of long, narrow tables covered with white cloth and decorated with white candles and white gladioli. Grandmother

Martin baked a tall wedding cake, which Mother was sure contained the finest nuts and dried fruit in the country.

It was time for the wedding to begin and Jacob sat on the front bench beside Mother, who wore a new dress the colour of violets.

"It's the prettiest dress of them all," Jacob whispered to her.

The organist started to play, a quartet sang some hymns, and then the "Wedding March" resounded through the plain, simple church.

Jacob watched with amazement as Suzanna floated down the centre aisle in a film of blue. Shy Amsey, with his kindly smile and sparkling eyes, walked tall and straight in a shiny black suit with a collar so stiff he couldn't move his head.

A billow of white appeared around Lydia, who walked beside Father. She saw him and smiled. There was a sermon, but Jacob barely heard it.

"It's the best wedding in the world," Jacob whispered again to Mother. He shut his eyes and imagined a castle where Lydia and Amsey were the king and queen and where they had a pond so big that it could easily hold dozens of giant Canada geese and all their goslings.

One September day, soon after Lydia's wedding,

Jacob put on his new school shoes, pulled on clean pants and shirt and walked to the end of the lane, where the yellow schoolbus would stop for him.

Mother walked with him to be certain that the bus would stop.

Jacob was both excited and worried. Would Amos be on the bus? Would his old friend be sitting next to another boy? Would he even speak to him?

Mother looked down at Jacob. "I always miss you, Jakie, when you go back to school," she said. "I don't want you to grow up too fast."

What did Mother mean? Jacob wondered. But he didn't have time to think about it because the yellow bus was scrunching to a stop in front of them.

Jacob swung himself up the steps, waved goodbye to Mother and walked inside.

"Jakie!" a familiar voice called from a middle seat. "Come and sit with me."

It was Amos. His round face was beaming.

"I got a new riddle from my cousins in Alberta," he laughed when Jacob slid into the seat beside him. "You'll never guess the answer."

The bus took its familiar swing around the corner road and the boys banged together. They laughed so loudly that the bus driver had to turn around and tell them to be quiet.

It was a good day at school. At recess time Jacob told Amos about the geese and asked him to come and see them soon. Amos promised he would. Jacob didn't say anything about Little Giant, though. Amos might laugh at him if he told him how much he loved the smallest gosling. They giggled together about not catching the mile-long pike.

"Dropping that pole was the dumbest thing you ever did, Jakie," Amos said.

Jacob half-heartedly agreed.

It was only later that he realized something. Not once during the school day had he worried about being the smallest boy in his class.

Early October came with crisp nights and a full, hazy moon. The leaves and stems of the potato plants shrivelled and died. Father, Orie and John unearthed rows of big, round potatoes with the large, red, mechanical harvester. Jacob helped on Saturdays by standing on a back platform and throwing out the stones that appeared on the moving belt that carried the newly dug potatoes into a nearby truck.

Jacob missed Lydia, but he liked visiting her farm, and Amsey had become his friend. John was back at university studying agriculture. Suzanna still zipped off to her hospital every morning. Mother's cheeks flushed with the hard work she was doing, storing food for the coming winter.

The sun that had burned through the summer began to mellow. It fringed the scarlet maple and the yellow willow leaves with gold.

Early one frosty morning a wild honking filled the sky. Migration time had come, and a wedge of Canada geese shot like an arrow across the rising sun. They were flying to the warm lands of the south. Jacob jumped from his bed and stood at the half-open bedroom window.

From the pond, his giant Canadas were bugling in reply. For a moment Jacob wanted to run to the pond and catch Little Giant in his arms and hold him tight. Then he saw his other giants, one by one, stroking their wings steadily upward. Little Giant was far behind.

Jacob called softly, "Try harder, Little Giant. You can make it."

Little Giant did stroke his wings harder and faster, and he roared by Jacob's window. He honked and honked, high and shrill.

"I'll be back in the spring...." he seemed to be saying to Jacob.

Little Giant caught up with the flock and joined his family far above the earth. The lead gander pointed his long neck south, and the wedge of geese stretched out into long, thin lines behind him.

Jacob knew that Little Giant would fly behind his father. He would feel the lift of the air as it flowed over his body. It was easier to fly one behind the other. Jacob had read this in John's book. Only the gander at the lead had to break through the air unaided. The geese would fly hundred of miles over rivers and forests and mountains. Hunters would shoot at them. Storms would strike them. But many would live and return to their nesting grounds when winter ended in the north. Some giant Canadas would nest in Ontario and some would come back to the Snyder pond.

Jacob listened to the faraway cries and honkings, and he could still hear Little Giant, "I'll be back in the spring...."

For a moment Jacob imagined that his arms were growing into wings and that he was flying from the window and up towards the rising sun. He looked down, expecting to see webbed feet. But he was barefoot and he counted ten toes and they were flat on the bedroom floor.

"Mother's facts and my fancies," he laughed and jumped back into bed. He snuggled under the warm feather-ticked blanket and was soon asleep again.

That evening at the Snyder home there was a guest for dinner. It was Mr McLean from the Natural Resources office. Jacob was surprised. Why was he here? He couldn't inspect the geese again because they had all flown away.

"Hello, Jacob" he smiled. "I came over to tell you something, and your mother invited me to stay for dinner."

Jacob waited. Everyone in his family except Lydia was sitting around the dinner table, and they all looked at him.

Mr McLean surveyed each face and then stopped at Jacob's.

"I want to especially thank you, Jacob," he said, "for doing an excellent job raising the giant geese this summer. Your family should be proud of you. You did the best job of all the co-operators, and your father tells me that you did almost all of it yourself. The little gosling might have died if you hadn't been there when he was shot."

"You're right about Jacob," John agreed.

Jacob sat up tall and straight on his high stool.

"Well," muttered Orie, clearing his throat as

he helped himself to a great mound of mashed potatoes, "I guess we'll have to stop calling you 'little Jakie.'"

Mother wiped her eyes and Jacob knew that she was sad because he was growing up. But he didn't mind.

Suzanna winked at him and made no attempt to squeeze and hug and kiss him in front of everybody.

Father smiled and said quietly, "God works in a mysterious way His wonders to perform."

Jacob felt warm and good inside. He looked out the window at the evening sky that was streaked with red and gold colours from the sinking sun. He thought of Little Giant shooting through the colours like a flaming arrow.

Orie pushed the extra dish of mashed potatoes in front of him and Jacob took a large helping. There was a long silence while everyone ate heartily.

"I know what I'm going to do next week," Jacob announced, gulping down a glass of milk to clear his throat. "I'm going to catch that mile-long pike with Amos."

Note to the Reader

The characters in this story are all make-believe, but the parts about the geese are true. Until 1962, it was thought in Canada that giant Canada geese, the largest geese in the world, had become extinct. Then some of them were discovered in Michigan and North Dakota. Long ago, their first nesting grounds had been in southwestern Ontario, the Canadian prairies and the north central United States.

The Ontario Department of Lands and Forests and the Ontario Waterfowl Research Foundation in Guelph, Ontario, decided to raise these giant geese again all across southern Ontario. They purchased some from a game farm in Michigan. After several years in captivity, pairs of them that had mated and were ready to raise families were given to southern Ontario farmers who had good nesting grounds. These farmers were called co-operators. This is how the geese in this story arrived at the Snyder farm. No hunting was allowed, so the geese population could grow.

There is a real Snyder potato farm on Beaverdale Road near the Ministry of Natural Resources office in southern Ontario. A pair of giant geese were placed on the pond there in the spring of 1969. Today hundreds of giant Canada geese can be seen in the summer and fall swimming over the real Snyder pond nibbling on the blue grass, which was planted there just for them,

The co-operators' program was so successful that the Natural Resources office on Beaverdale Road encourages hunting and has even extended the season. But the real Mr Snyder, who is affectionately called Mr Spud and who has this name on the licence plate of his car, has posted a "no hunting" sign on his pond. He would rather watch than eat his geese.

The author wishes to thank Ed G. Snyder, the real potato farmer, and his nephew, John Snyder, a minister and also a farmer, who helped her often with innumerable details in writing this story.